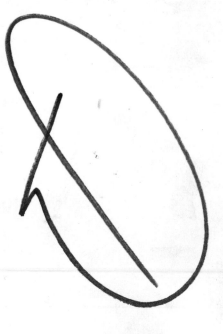

THE BASEBALL TRICK

THE
BASEBALL TRICK

by SCOTT CORBETT

Illustrated by Paul Galdone

 An Atlantic Monthly Press Book

Little, Brown and Company Boston · Toronto

ATLANTIC–LITTLE, BROWN BOOKS
ARE PUBLISHED BY
LITTLE, BROWN AND COMPANY
IN ASSOCIATION WITH
THE ATLANTIC MONTHLY PRESS

*Published simultaneously in Canada
by Little, Brown & Company (Canada) Limited*

PRINTED IN THE UNITED STATES OF AMERICA

THE BASEBALL TRICK

To Fenton

1

BUMPS had two words to describe baseball pitchers.

"All pitchers are temper mental," he told Kerby as they sat in their private clubhouse talking over the 8-0 win Fenton Claypool had pitched for their sandlot team. "Temper mental. Moody. Now you take Fenton. Doing ordinary things, you couldn't ask for anybody with an evener temper. Always nice, never sore about nothing. Steady as a rock. But put a glove on him and send him out to the pitcher's mound, and what is he?"

Bumps reached out and tapped Kerby on the chest with two powerful fingers.

"Temper mental, that's what."

Kerby knew the two words should really be one — "temperamental" — but Bumps Burton was not a fellow you went around correcting, not if you cared about the condition of your nose. Those same two powerful fingers had a way of becoming a steel clamp whenever their chunky owner grew annoyed.

It was a long time since Bumps had given Kerby's nose a good twist. They were pals now, and fellow members of the most exclusive club in the neighborhood. Fenton was the only other member. But there was no point in straining friendship, and besides, Kerby had more important things to worry about than Bumps's vocabulary. He had Fenton to worry about.

"He's temper mental, all right," he agreed. "I can't get over it."

Imagine Fenton Claypool being so mad he would not even stop at their clubhouse with them after the game! It was not as if the clubhouse was not handy, either. It stood in the vacant lot behind Kerby's house and between Bumps's and Fenton's. Yet when they reached home Fenton had stalked away across the lot straight to his house, with his glove in his hand and his bat on his shoulder. And before he went inside he threw the bat down and gave it a good kick, which was a mistake. He must have caught his toe wrong, because he jumped around holding it, and then went limping into the house, banging the screen door behind him.

Bumps sighed.

"You'd think he'd be satisfied. He pitched a beautiful shutout, didn't he? But just because he can't ever get a hit himself, he's sore."

They played seven-inning games. After striking out for

4

the third time, in the bottom of the sixth with the bases loaded, Fenton had been so mad he struck out the opposing side in the seventh to end the game.

"He had such good stuff I couldn't hardly hold on to it," said Bumps, who was their catcher. "But even that didn't make him feel better. All pitchers are that way. They all want to be hitters. Let 'em hit even a dribbly little single, and that's all they talk about after the game. 'How did you like that base knock I got?' they ask everybody. They're all alike. I tell you, if there was some way I could have let Fenton hit one of my homers, I would have, just so's he'd stop bellyaching."

The three of them were sitting inside their new clubhouse. Bumps, Kerby, and Waldo, that is. With Fenton absent, there was room for Waldo to sit inside.

Waldo was a tousle-haired combination of several good breeds of dog. He was still young enough to be part puppy at times, though very grown up at others. Kerby seldom went anywhere without him.

When everyone was present at the clubhouse, Waldo had to sit outside. This annoyed him, because he considered himself a full member of the club. But today he was inside, and very pleased with himself. He nuzzled Kerby, and his wagging tail banged a tattoo of affection on the wall.

"Easy, Waldo! Oh — I forgot," said Kerby, and Bumps laughed.

"Sure, it's okay now, Waldo." Bumps slapped the flat of his hand approvingly against the sturdy boards. Before their old clubhouse had collapsed in a splintery heap during their battle with Red Blake and his gang, things had been different. If Waldo had banged his tail against the wall then, the whole clubhouse would have trembled. But old Mr. Carmody, who owned the vacant lot, had let them build a new clubhouse. "Build it right this time!" he had ordered, waggling his cane at them, and they did. But because they had liked the old clubhouse, they had built the new one the same size, and with the same sort of small door you had to crawl in and out of.

Waldo gave the wall of few more thumps and then stopped. He cocked his head to one side, assumed his version of a fierce look, and became Waldo the Watchdog. He uttered a low growl.

"Someone must be coming," said Kerby.

Bang! bang! bang!

They winced, because it made a terrible racket inside the clubhouse when somebody kicked it outside. Waldo let out a sharp bark that nearly finished deafening them, and stuck his head out the door. Kerby pushed him on through the doorway

6

and they crawled outside, Bumps first. Being club president, Bumps always crawled in and out first.

Thanks to Waldo's noisy protest, their visitors had retreated a few steps. A large redheaded boy stood flanked by two smaller boys, watching with a cocky expression as they appeared. It was Red Blake and two of his gang, Eddie Mumford and Buzzy Dugan.

Bumps thrust his heavy jaw quite a distance in Red Blake's direction.

"What's the big idea of kicking our clubhouse?"

Red assumed a mocking expression of wounded innocence.

"Kicking it? Who was kicking? I was knocking."

"You were kicking."

"Knocking."

"Kicking. Think I don't know the difference between a kick and a knock? Just keep your feet off the woodwork, that's all," growled Bumps, inspecting the boards for marks. "Whatcha want around here, anyway?"

"We hear you beat the Cougars today."

"Natcherly."

"We're playing them tomorrow. We'll beat 'em twice as bad."

They stared at Red Blake's arrogant freckled face.

"Who's we?"

"The Wildcats. We've got a team now, too."

"Oh. Sure. I heard you were trying to start one with that bunch of butterfingers over in your neighborhood."

Red glanced left and right, exchanging smirks with his henchmen.

"Oh, did you hear the nasty thing he called us, fellows?" he mocked in a prissy voice. "Butterfingers! I think I'm gonna cry."

"Me, too. Boo-hoo!" said Eddie Mumford, who was always heavy-handed with the wit.

"Well," Red continued, "us bunch of butterfingers are here to challenge you Panthers to a game Friday, unless you're afraid to play us."

Bumps was genuinely surprised at such presumption.

"Don't you want to practice a little more first?" he suggested. "Say four or five years?"

But Red responded with a confident snicker.

"By the time we take care of the Cougars, we'll be practiced up more than *you* guys can handle!"

Bumps spat on the ground between them and shook his head wonderingly.

"Well, if it's having your ears pounded off in a ball game you're looking for, we're willing."

"Okay. See you Friday morning at the school field."

"Be a pleasure."

The club members watched their rivals turn and swagger away, snickering and talking under their breath and elbowing each other. Not until the others were out of sight up the block did Kerby and Bumps permit themselves to change expression. Not until then did Bumps allow a worried look to creep onto his large and ordinarily stolid face. He turned puzzled eyes toward Kerby.

"I don't like it," he admitted. "Those guys are really sure of themselves. They got something up their sleeves."

"If you ask me," said Kerby, "we'd better scout their game with the Cougars!"

2

BUMPS picked up his catcher's equipment and said he guessed he'd head for home before his old lady started hollering for him.

Shouldering his bat, with his fielder's glove strung on it, Kerby Maxwell headed thoughtfully for the loose board in the fence that separated his own back yard from the vacant lot.

Waldo was the only one of the three of them whose horizon remained unclouded. Trotting along beside Kerby, he glanced over in the direction of Xerxes's house, and it was obvious what he was thinking. He was thinking it might be pleasant to give the big yellow cat some exercise, if he happened to be outside, and he was wondering if Mrs. Pembroke was around.

Xerxes lived next door with Mrs. Pembroke, and Waldo had learned that it paid to check up on her whereabouts before chasing her cat. The best time to exercise Xerxes was when Mrs. Pembroke was elsewhere. She had a voice that hurt

Waldo's ears, and she was also a good hand with a broom.

When they had pushed the loose board aside and stepped into their own backyard, Waldo trotted over to the thin place in the hedge, where he could look through into the next backyard. His brown eyes brightened, and he glanced over his shoulder at Kerby with his tongue lollygagging happily out of the side of his mouth. Kerby stooped down for a look. Xerxes was curled up on the lawn, fast asleep.

Waldo was a generous dog who liked to share his pleasures. It was always more fun to chase Xerxes up a tree when Kerby was there to give the order in a low voice — "Sic 'im!"

"Sic —" began Kerby, but before he could finish, a frightful noise seemed to make the very ground shake. Xerxes shot straight up into the air with a yowl of terror. Waldo broke the

backward standing broad jump record for dogs. Kerby, still stooped down, fell over backward.

"RUFF! RUFF! RUFF-F-F!"

It was like all the barking they had ever heard rolled into one huge outburst. Kerby caught a blurred glimpse of a streak of yellow heading for a tree followed by an enormous galumphing monster, and then Xerxes appeared high in the branches of a tree while the deep-throated barking continued below.

After his first start of surprise, Waldo's reaction was one of outrage. A strange dog chasing *his* cat up one of *their* trees! — such an outrage was not to be tolerated for an instant. Courageously Waldo charged through the thin place in the hedge.

"R-R-R-R-OWF!"

Waldo must have left skid marks on Mrs. Pembroke's lawn, so quickly did he reappear in his own yard. His bulging eyes, when they met Kerby's, said more plainly than words, "He's *big!*"

"Come on, boy, let's go inside," said Kerby anxiously. "Gee, I wonder where *he* came from?"

Across the way the back door opened, and Mrs. Pembroke began scolding the intruder in a voice that would have made even the Hound of the Baskervilles put its tail between its legs and retreat. Kerby heard the strange dog go crashing away through the shrubbery, sounding at least as big as a moose. He held their back screen door open for Waldo and watched him slink inside.

"Cheer up, maybe he's just visiting. Maybe he won't come back again."

But Waldo was not to be comforted by any such shallow optimism. He slurped a few tonguefuls mournfully from his water dish and then flopped down on the kitchen floor with his head resting broodingly on his forepaws. Kerby threw up his hands in protest.

"Fenton's not enough!" he complained. "Now I've got a worried dog on my hands, too!"

Grumpily he took his bat and glove down to the basement,

14

where he had a corner allotted to him for all his stuff. There he sat down on a box to think about his many problems.

Fenton was still the worst one. If Fenton kept worrying so much about his hitting, it might start to affect his pitching — and now that they had a game scheduled with a disturbingly confident Red Blake and his gang, that could be disastrous. If there were only some way to help Fenton get a hit! But there was no doubt about it, and no use pretending — Fenton was just about the worst excuse for a hitter who ever stepped up to the plate.

Misery loves company. Waldo proved it by padding down the basement stairs to join Kerby. Still as tragic a figure as ever, Waldo skulked across the basement and lay down beside a large wooden chest Kerby had been given years ago to keep all his old toys in.

"Oh, stop thinking about that big mutt," ordered Kerby, but he was not devoting his full attention to Waldo's worries. Slowly his gaze was centering on the toy chest, and temptation was beckoning. Did the answer to Fenton's difficulties lie inside that chest?

After a moment Kerby went over and opened it. All that met the eye inside was a jumble of wooden building blocks, with which he had built many a fort and castle in his younger days. But when he pushed them aside and dug underneath them, something else came to view: a long wooden box that looked shabby and quite old. Kerby lifted it out and carried it to the workbench.

Inside the plain lid, as he opened the box, faded printing appeared in red and black letters:

FEATS O' MAGIC CHEMISTRY SET

Instructive! Entertaining!
Hours of Amusement!
Astonish Your Friends!
Entertain at Parties!
Make Extra Money Giving Demonstrations!

Corked glass tubes with dim labels were ranged in a row. Other sections in the box held eyedroppers and glass containers with measurements on their sides. A booklet was there, too. Its cover claimed it described *One Thousand and One Tricks to Do with Your FEATS O' MAGIC Chemistry Set.*

Kerby had been given this box by a mysterious friend named Mrs. Graymalkin, whom he had helped in the park once when she had the high heel of her shoe caught in the drain by the drinking fountain. She said the chemistry set had belonged to her son Felix when he was a little boy. Though it was old, many of the tubes still contained chemicals, and

16

Kerby knew from experience that it was no ordinary chemistry set. Some strange experiments had resulted when he used it.

Kerby thumbed through the booklet, wondering if one of the one thousand and one tricks might help the world's worst hitter get a hit, but he soon gave up. The booklet only talked about stuff like pouring two colorless chemicals together and getting a red liquid. Tricks like that were small-time magic, compared to what Mrs. Graymalkin had come up with in the way of suggestions. Should he go look for her in the park and ask her for help?

Kerby closed the box, and his fingers drummed on it as he considered this temptation, but then he resisted it. Wouldn't do any good, anyway. Fenton was too smart. He would catch on, and he wouldn't approve. Kerby remembered how Fenton had felt about the chemical that helped Kerby write a poem. He had felt that using it was taking an unfair advantage. And he had been right! Certainly Kerby did not want to repeat *that* sort of experience. Sighing, he closed the chemistry set and put it back in its hiding place, under the blocks in his toy chest, and went upstairs. A dejected Waldo followed him.

As far as Fenton's problem was concerned, the next best thing to Mrs. Graymalkin's help that Kerby could think of was to talk to his father about it. He brought up the subject at supper.

"Fenton's a great pitcher, but he can't hit," said Kerby, "and he'd rather get a hit than anything."

"Same old story," said Mr. Maxwell. "I remember a kid named Fizzle Foster that used to pitch for our team when I was a boy. One time he hit a home run, and I thought we'd never hear the end of it."

"That's the way it is with Fenton. Or it would be, if he ever got a hit. All he thinks about is getting one. I wish he could, so he'd shut up about it."

"What seems to be his trouble?"

"Well, for one thing, Bumps says it's because he always tries to kill the ball. He swings too hard."

"Yes, most poor hitters do that."

"Bumps tells him, why try to kill the ball, when you can't even hurt its feelings? But Fenton won't listen."

Kerby's father sat back in his chair.

"Well, I'd have to see Fenton in action before I could suggest anything that might help. Tell you what. I'll have a little free time in the morning, before a ten o'clock appointment. Maybe we can get out, you and Bumps and Fenton and I, and have a look at his style. Maybe I can spot something."

"That would be great, Pop," said Kerby, feeling that things

were looking up. He glanced at Waldo, over in his corner of the dining room. In ordinary circumstances Waldo would have looked pleased, too, because he was an intelligent dog and always seemed to sense the way things were going. But in this instance, Waldo merely rolled up one eye mournfully and then let it droop again. He looked like some old hound grieving to death at his master's grave. Kerby shook his head. Something would certainly have to be done about Waldo!

3

WHILE his father was finishing his breakfast coffee, Kerby ran over to Fenton's house.

"Come on, Waldo," he called as he left, and Waldo came, but he was not the companion Kerby was used to. There was no spring in his step, no frisk in his tail. He had not even had a good night's sleep. Kerby was sure of that. He had heard Waldo up, pacing the floor, just before he himself had gone to sleep.

At least Fenton looked more like his old self when he came to the back door. His solemn face, framed by its cup-handle ears, was no longer sullen. Fenton Claypool was a tall, thin boy who stood very straight and who tended to think very straight about everything except getting a hit in baseball. Where everything else was concerned, he had quite a scientific mind and high standards of conduct. Kerby supposed everybody had to be childish about one thing in life.

"Hey, can you come out, Fenton?"

"Sure, why?"

"Well, Bumps and I have some news to tell you about Red Blake, and besides that my dad is coming out for a while before he has to go to work, and we're going to play a little catch or something."

Kerby knew he had to be diplomatic about getting his friend to join them, because Fenton was sensitive about his hitting problem.

"Okay, I'll be there in a couple of minutes."

"Great. I'll get Bumps."

Bumps came right out when Kerby told him what was up. By that time Mr. Maxwell had appeared. They were able to talk about Fenton's difficulties for a minute before Fenton showed up.

"Kerby can throw a few to Fenton, and then you can see what he does, Mr. Maxwell," said Bumps. "Come on, Kerby, I'll warm you up."

"Okay, Bumps." Kerby moved back toward the street, Bumps put on his mask, and Kerby began to throw in a few pitches.

"Look at that, Mr. Maxwell. Every pitch a gopher ball. Kerby's a good second baseman, but he's no pitcher. I could hit his stuff a mile," said Bumps. "Almost anybody could. But wait till you see Fenton."

The vacant lot was not large. The houses on the other side

of the street seemed dangerously close. Mr. Maxwell eyed them dubiously.

"Do you think it's safe to have batting practice here?"

His question caused such merriment that Kerby had to stop throwing for a minute.

"With *Fenton* batting?" he cried.

"Listen, Mr. Maxwell, I'll pay for every window Fenton busts with my own money from mowing lawns!" Bumps assured him with a yawp of laughter. "If he even gets a foul tip I'll fall over in a faint!"

Fenton's back door opened, and they pulled themselves together, not wanting him to know what they were laughing about. By the time Fenton got there, they were all looking very serious.

"Good morning, Mr. Maxwell." Where most boys would have said, "Hi," Fenton said, "Good morning." He was always very polite, and yet he was never sticky about it. Coming from Fenton, not even Bumps minded politeness.

"Good morning, Fenton. I hear you pitched quite a game yesterday."

Fenton shrugged. "It was okay, I guess."

"I should think an eight-to-nothing shutout *was* okay. I understand you've been in a hitting slump, though."

Fenton's solemn face acknowledged this understatement of the century with a brief, dismal grin.

23

"Mr. Maxwell, I've never been *out* of one."

"That so? Hmm." Kerby's father picked up a bat and waved it around reflectively. "When I was a boy, our pitcher had that problem, too. Pitcher by the name of Fizzle Foster, a southpaw with a great fireball. I used to try to help him work on his hitting, and I remember one time when he finally got two singles in one game."

"Two singles in one game?" said Fenton, awed. For someone like Bumps, a mere two singles would have been a bad day at the plate, but for a pitcher like Fenton it was terrific.

"That's right." Mr. Maxwell handed the bat to Fenton. "Tell you what. Let me see you take a cut at a few, and maybe I can suggest something."

Fenton's quick glance, taking in Bumps and Kerby, made it plain that he was not fooled. He knew they had arranged the whole thing. But now that he was there, he was too polite to refuse. Besides, he was only human. Hope sprang as eternally in his breast as in the next one. If Mr. Maxwell was able to help Fizzle Foster, maybe he could help him, too.

"Okay, Mr. Maxwell," he said manfully, even though he looked a trifle pink from embarrassment. Grasping the bat, he stepped up to the plate Bumps had marked out on the ground. Then he hesitated, with a look of concern. "If I hit one here, I'm liable to break a window."

24

"I'll pay for it," said Mr. Maxwell and Bumps at practically the same instant. They exchanged a poker-faced glance.

"We'll split it," suggested Mr. Maxwell.

"Okay," said Bumps, and squatted behind the plate. "Let's go, Kerby."

Fenton went into a lethal crouch, swishing the bat back and forth fiercely, tense from head to foot. A green pitcher who didn't know him might have been terrified. Kerby, however, put a fat one straight across the plate. If Bumps had been doing the batting, the ball would probably have broken a window in the *next* block.

WHISH!

Fenton had stirred a lot of air, but the ball was safely in Bumps's mitt. Nobody said anything. Bumps tossed the ball out, and Kerby pitched again.

WHISH!

And again.

WHISH!

And after each swing, Mr. Maxwell closed his eyes like a man in pain. No question about it, Fenton was terrible. Mr. Maxwell had seen people in wheelchairs who had better swings than Fenton's. By comparison, he made Fizzle Foster look like Willie Mays. After half a dozen pitches, Bumps glanced over his shoulder, and he and Mr. Maxwell exchanged

grim nods. In the meantime, however, Kerby's father had been doing some thinking. It was true that Fenton was trying to kill the ball, as Bumps had said, but it was also true that telling him so had not done any good. So Mr. Maxwell tried another approach.

"Easy, Fenton! That last swing was pretty close, and if you had connected, it would have cost Bumps and me a lot of money."

The way Fenton beamed when he heard this was downright pathetic.

"Just swing at them easy for a minute now, and let me watch without having to worry about the windows."

"Okay, Mr. Maxwell," said Fenton seriously.

Bumps was lucky. He had a mask on to hide his grin. Kerby had to turn away for a minute and pretend he was getting something out of his eye, before he could pitch again with a straight face.

Fenton still missed a couple more, even swinging easy, but then on the next one he hit a dribbler back to Kerby, and on the next one he hit a little pop fly that Kerby actually had to back up half a step to take.

Mr. Maxwell pretended to be impressed. As a matter of fact, he *was* impressed, because he had begun to wonder if Fenton could hit *anything*.

"You're meeting the ball nicely now," he declared. "And there's a lot to be said for that."

"Yes, but I couldn't get anywhere on little dribblers and pop flies like those," Fenton pointed out scornfully.

"Well, I don't know. Don't forget, Fenton," said Mr. Maxwell, delivering a sound sandlot baseball rule, "you have to hit the ball first before you can give the other team a chance to make an error."

Being of a scientific turn of mind, even Fenton had to admit that there was some truth in what Kerby's father said. But even so, it was plain he failed to find any satisfaction in the idea.

4

"I'VE been thinking over what Kerby's pop said," declared Bumps, after Mr. Maxwell had left, "and I think he's got something, Fenton."

Fenton gave them one of his level-eyed looks.

"You guys aren't fooling me."

"Well, gee, Fenton, we're only trying to help your hitting," admitted Kerby. "We thought my dad might be able to spot something. And you've got to admit he did."

"But I don't want to just hit dribbles to the infield," said Fenton the dreamer. "I want to smack a few through the infield into deep right, or center."

"Now, listen, Fenton," said Bumps, in a somewhat exasperated tone, "stop worrying about hitting 'em through the infield. How about hitting a few *into* the infield, for a starter?"

"That's right," agreed Kerby. "You've got to begin somewhere."

That old sullen look was coming back on their pitcher's face.

"Well, I'll think it over," he said, but he did not sound convinced. He was still dreaming of screaming line drives. Kerby decided it was time to change the subject.

"Okay, think it over. But we've got something else to think over, too," he said, with a glance at Bumps. "Something about Red Blake and his Wildcats."

"His what?"

"I guess I better call a meeting," said Bumps.

Wonderingly, Fenton crawled into the clubhouse behind them. As for Waldo, he took up his post outside. It was just one more blow to his self-esteem, but he did not have enough spirit that morning to look indignant. His head sank onto his paws with an air of gloomy self-contempt, as if he felt he did not deserve to be inside any more.

"Meeting will come to order," said Bumps. "Now, what happened is this . . ."

And he told Fenton all about Red Blake's challenge. Fenton listened with increasing thoughtfulness.

"It does sound as if he's got something up his sleeve," he said, nodding. "And I agree we'd better scout that game today and have a look at his team."

"When you think of the guys that live over in Red's neighborhood, I can't see how they could be so great. Eddie Mumford and Bruce Carmichael and Moony Davis —"

30

"Yes, and Butterfingers Blatweiler," added Fenton. "I can't see it, either."

"Red's a good pitcher," said Kerby.

"No better 'n Fenton."

"Well, we'll see," said Fenton.

"You guys will have to do the scouting," Bumps said, "on account of I promised Mrs. Scofield I'd mow her lawn this afternoon, and she's a regular customer I can't disappoint."

From outside came a deep, thunder-like rumble that made them jump.

"There's that big dog again!" said Kerby, and hastily crawled out. Waldo had sprung to his feet and was looking in the direction of Mrs. Pembroke's house with helpless indignation. By the time Kerby got outside, Xerxes was high in a tree, and the sound of underbrush being trampled indicated that the intruder was already continuing on his way.

"Golly!" said Kerby, who could not help being impressed. "He put Xerxes up the tree with one bark!"

It was an unfortunate remark. It only rubbed in the situation, as far as Waldo was concerned. He hung his head and refused to meet Kerby's sympathetic eye. Instead he started walking away toward home. A pitcher who had been knocked out of the box could not have looked more woebegone.

"I guess Waldo wants to go inside," said Kerby. "I'd better go let him in."

Actually, with a monstrous dog like that wandering around loose, he was concerned for Waldo's safety. He followed his friend to the fence and pushed the board aside for him. Together they went into their own backyard. In the meantime, Kerby had noticed, Xerxes was coming down out of the tree. By the time they were passing the thin place in the hedge, Xerxes was in his yard again.

Waldo and Kerby stopped to look through at Xerxes. The big yellow cat paused to look back at them. For a moment he and Waldo exchanged an unhappy stare, and then Xerxes let out a small, heartbroken meow. There was no mistaking the catch in his voice as he went on to his back door and scratched to be let in. Anyone could see that as far as Xerxes was concerned, it just wasn't any fun to be out in the backyard anymore.

Bergmeyer Avenue ran up the hill past the school field. Alongside the sidewalk there was a low stone wall people could lean on when they stopped to watch a game down on the field.

"We can stand up here and look as if we just happened to be passing by, huh?" said Kerby. Fenton smiled and shook his head.

"If he sees us up here — and he'll be looking for us — Red Blake won't be fooled. But at least this way we can look them over first without having to listen to his yak. Then after a while we can go down and let him talk."

The game was just getting under way, with the Cougars in the field and Red Blake's Wildcats at bat.

"That's Pinky Marshall batting. He's pretty good."

Pinky proved it by getting a hit. Eddie Mumford came up next, and struck out, much to Kerby's satisfaction.

"They're not so hot," he mocked, but Fenton reminded him it was pretty early to say that yet. To their surprise, Red Blake strode to the plate next.

"That's funny. I'd have figured him to bat fourth, in the clean-up spot, instead of third."

"So would I. He must be about their best hitter."

Red smacked another single, Pinky went to third, and the clean-up man appeared. The onlookers exchanged a blank glance.

"Who's that?"

"Never saw him before!"

The boy batting fourth was big, even bigger than Bumps Burton. He looked like somebody who should have been in high school for a while. He was swinging three bats, and when he tossed away two of them he waggled the other one around as if it were a toothpick. They could practically see the Cougar pitcher gulp from where they were standing. But he wound up, and pitched.

34

CRACK!

The stranger hit the first pitch. Kerby's and Fenton's heads swiveled slowly from left to right, watching the ball travel.

"Wow! That's farther than I've ever seen Bumps hit one!"

They watched the stranger round the bases at a hulking trot while the outfielders chased the ball. It was an easy home run.

"Hey! And who's this?"

Another boy they did not know had come to the plate to bat fifth. He was almost as big as the clean-up batter.

"What's going on here?" Kerby demanded angrily.

While they watched with sinking hearts, the second big stranger got a hit and was followed by a third stranger, who hit another homer. Then a boy they knew got a double. Only then, in the eighth and ninth spots, did Bruce Carmichael and Buzzy Dugan bat. Bruce popped up, and Buzzy hit an easy one-hopper to second to end the inning. But five runs had crossed the plate. And Moony Davis and Butterfingers Blatweiler, boys from Red's own block who should have been playing, were sitting unhappily on the bench.

"Where did those new guys come from?"

"I don't know, but we'll find out," said Fenton grimly. "Let's watch a while longer, though. I want to see how they look in the field."

And then he added a pitcher's envious comment.

"Might know that Red would not only be a good pitcher, but a good hitter, too!"

The Cougars came in to bat, and the Wildcats trotted out to their positions in the field. Red Blake began to throw in his warm-up pitches.

"Look who's behind the plate. It's that big lug that's batting clean-up."

"Yes, and those other two guys are in center and right."

The lead-off batter stepped in. Red threw his first pitch. It was a beauty.

"Stee-rike!" The umpire's arm went up. An old retired railroad man named Mr. Caldwell was umpiring, as usual. He lived right across the street from the field. He loved to umpire, and always came over when there was a game. He even had a blue umpire's cap and a mask and a chest protector.

Red struck out the first batter on three straight strikes. The next batter grounded out. The third batter worked Red for a walk. That brought up Maxie Klein, the Cougars' clean-up man, and they knew Maxie was good.

"Let's see what Maxie can do with him," growled Kerby in a hopeful tone. "He even got a hit off *you* yesterday."

Maxie let one go by, and then their hearts lifted with the ball as he really unloaded on a fat pitch. The ball headed deep toward right center . . .

36

"Would you look at that!"

Running like the wind, the centerfielder had raced back and taken it with one hand for the third out.

By the middle of the fourth inning, the score was 16-0. When Red came off the mound he looked up and waved at them mockingly.

"Hi, fellas!" he shouted. "Enjoying the game?"

"I knew he spotted us, long before now," muttered Fenton. "Well, let's go down and ask a couple of questions."

"Like why are those strangers playing instead of Moony and Butterfingers!"

They vaulted the wall and ran down the slope onto the field. Sitting on the bench, Red turned around and watched them. Finally he got up and came to meet them.

"How do you like the Wildcats?"

Fenton wasted no time on small talk.

"How come Moony and Butterfingers aren't playing? And where are a couple of other boys from your neighborhood that anybody would expect to see on your team?"

Red acted surprised at the question.

"Why, some of the new guys in our neighborhood are better, so Moony and Butterfingers are our substitutes now."

"What do you mean, new guys?"

"Well, for instance, our catcher is Pinky Marshall's cousin that's come to stay at Pinky's for the summer."

"What about those two outfielders?"

"Freddie and Ferdie? They're cousins. New kids in the neighborhood." Red stared at Fenton and Kerby with his upper lip lifted arrogantly. "What's the matter, don't you want to play us anymore? If you're chicken just because we've got some new guys, why, just say so."

Sure, and never hear the end of Red telling everybody about it, thought Kerby. Fenton was obviously thinking the same thing, because he said, "Don't worry. We'll play you, all right."

"Okay. Tomorrow afternoon, right here," said Red with a complacent laugh, all but licking his lips. He waved his hand grandly at the bleachers that stood on the third base side of the diamond. "Stick around. Enjoy the game!"

"No, thanks. We've got better things to do. Come on, Kerby," said Fenton, and turned to lead the way back up the slope. Behind them, Red's nasty snicker sped them on their way.

5

TO HELP themselves over this unpleasant new turn of events, they crossed the street to Doc Browley's candy store and bought a candy bar apiece. They stood around outside, eating them. Fenton paced up and down, thinking, while he munched.

"There's not much time to find out more about those guys, but I wish we could," he said. "I don't trust Red."

"Neither do I."

"But it's hard to find out anything on such short notice."

They finished their candy bars in silence. It was a melancholy feast, but it made them feel better.

"Tell you what," said Fenton. "Let's have one more look to see how the game is going before we head for home. But we won't let Red see us this time. Let's cross over to the big tree and watch from behind it."

Alongside the low wall at one point an old elm towered above the sidewalk. If they were careful they could peep at the ball game from behind it without being seen by Red

Blake or any of his pals. They crossed the street opposite the tree, and kept it between them and Red's line of vision. When they had reached it, Fenton craned his neck cautiously around one side of the trunk, while Kerby kept out of sight.

"That centerfielder of theirs is up again," he reported.

CRACK!

Fenton groaned. "He hit it a mile."

Kerby groaned. "You're telling me. I got ears."

"It's another homer."

The next batter got another hit.

"Now Bruce Carmichael is up."

A less authoritative crack was soon heard.

"He popped up again."

"Good."

"Looks as if that's the end of the inning. Well, I suppose we might as well . . ."

Fenton paused in the midst of turning away.

"Wait a minute."

"What's the matter?"

Fenton held up his hand. He was watching and listening intently. After a moment he reported.

"Red walked out to the mound, and that centerfielder yelled to him that he and his cousin have to go home. He said, 'Let those guys play now,' and Moony and Butterfingers are taking their places. And now Freddie and Ferdie are leaving."

41

Fenton's eyes narrowed as he glanced around at Kerby.

"Here's our chance!"

"What chance?"

"Let's follow those two and see where they live!"

"Oh! Good idea!"

"We'll be careful following them, but probably they never even noticed us when we went down on the field. Come on! Let's get across the street — they're coming this way."

Fenton led the way back to Doc Browley's candy store, explaining, "Let's get out of sight, for now."

They ducked into the candy store and stood tensely watching the wall, where the cousins would appear when they had climbed the slope.

"Want something, boys?"

"Sure, Doc," said Fenton promptly. "I'd like two cents' worth of jujubes, please." He was very good at thinking on his feet that way.

Doc stooped and opened the penny candy case's sliding door. His little trowel dug into the jujubes. At that instant two heads appeared above the wall.

"Here they come!" muttered Kerby.

The cousins climbed over the wall, crossed the street, and headed down it in the other direction.

"We'll be back for them later, Doc!" Fenton cried, and

they left the plump little man stooped over his jujubes with a surprised look on his face.

Half a block behind the cousins, who were sauntering along in a relaxed manner, Fenton and Kerby speculated as to what was their best strategy.

"If we keep ducking in doorways and stuff like that, they may notice and get suspicious," Fenton pointed out. "I think the best thing we can do is walk along bold as brass, as if we didn't even know they were there. That way they'll never pay any attention to us."

"You mean, just walk along?"

"That's right. Just walk along. Laughing and talking."

So they just walked along, laughing and talking. Some of their laughing and talking was pretty strained, but nevertheless it worked. The cousins never so much as glanced around at them.

Waldo was not present, of course. He had stayed home, moping. Kerby missed him, but in a way he was just as glad Waldo was not with them at the moment. They were less conspicuous without him romping along.

In a very short time they were nearing the limits of any area that could conceivably be counted as part of Red Blake's neighborhood. In fact, they were getting close to Gorman Square. And still the cousins walked on.

Another block, and they had reached the square. Once there, the cousins did something unexpected. They ran for a bus and leaped aboard. As the bus pulled away, Fenton raced forward to the bus stop.

"Excuse me, sir," he said to a man who was waiting there, "can you tell me what bus that was that just left?"

"Sure, sonny. It was a Cullens Avenue bus."

"Thanks."

As Kerby ran up, Fenton turned to him with a grim face.

"How do you like that? They live so far away they have to take a Cullens Avenue bus to get home!"

They stared at each other with a glare of righteous indignation.

"That dirty crook Red Blake!" cried Kerby. "Those new guys are nothing but *ringers!*"

They were unquestionably ringers. They were boys from some other neighborhood entirely whom Red Blake had gotten to come play on his team.

"Okay, what are we going to do about it?"

Fenton admitted he had no ready answer.

"I don't know. Red Blake's no dummy. If we start talking tomorrow about what we just saw those cousins do, he'll say they had to go somewhere on some errand before they went home, and there won't be time to prove anything different."

"Well, let's think of *something*. Because we can't let him get away with it."

They had turned back and were on their way home now. They walked a few blocks in silence, while they both thought, especially Fenton. Kerby was doing his best, although he had not come up with anything very exciting as yet. They were getting close to home when an unexpected sight suddenly wrenched his attention in a new direction.

"Look! There's that big dog!"

"Where?"

"That girl has him on a leash!"

"Oh! Yes! Kerby, he *is* big!"

Up at the corner ahead of them a girl about their own age had appeared, tugged along by a creature so huge that passersby were all but springing out of the way to let him pass. Other dogs might bite postmen; this one looked as if he would eat them whole.

"Goodness gracious!" cried one old lady, stopping in her tracks as though paralyzed with fear. In a voice both boys would have described as gooey, the girl reassured her.

"Oh, don't worry, please, Gustavus wouldn't hurt anybody. He's really as gentle as can be."

"I'll bet," muttered Kerby.

"Are you sure that's the same dog, Kerby?"

"Sure I'm sure. I only got one look at him through the

hedge, but it's him, all right. Where are you going to find *two* dogs that size around here, for that matter?"

"No wonder poor Waldo was scared. I hope that girl and her dog are only visiting someone and not staying long."

"I hope so, too. But I don't think Waldo is going to get over it very fast. Or Xerxes, for that matter. I wish I could think of a way to scare off Gustavus, but he doesn't look like anything to fool with."

They watched the girl and the dog cross the street, and Fenton said, "Let's follow them. Maybe we can think of something."

They had not gone far when around the next corner came a man leading a toy Boston bull terrier.

"Hey, look at that! That man had better get out of the way if he wants to have any dog left!"

But the little dog had seen Gustavus, and his sudden lunge forward yanked his leash out of the man's hand. Yapping noisily, the toy terrier rushed straight at the enormous dog.

Gustavus looked down at him, let out one fearful howl — and ducked behind the girl, cowering. The man had already run up and retrieved his terrier's leash, and now he dragged him away.

"Now, now, Gustavus, it's all right," said the girl, soothing her pet. "He's still only a puppy, and he's very gentle," she told the man.

"I'm sorry about Buster here," he replied. "He's an old fellow, and nobody's ever told him he isn't the biggest dog around. Stop it, Buster! Down, sir!"

Fenton and Kerby had stopped to watch the encounter. Now they were staring at each other with their mouths open.

"Why, he's just a big softy! That bark of his is only noise," said Fenton.

But Kerby was scratching his head as though trying to dig an idea out of it.

"That's fine," he said, "but how can we explain that to Waldo?"

6

AS THEY walked on toward home, Fenton and Kerby
tried to think of some way to get the good news across to
Waldo.

"Waldo's smart. Maybe we can do it somehow."

"Maybe we'll have to take him for a walk, and let him see
for himself, if we can trail that girl and her dog again."

"If only he'd been along now!"

Down the street to their right, as they reached a corner,
they could see one end of Peterson Park. This was a small
public park where they often played, since it was not far from
their homes. More important, it was the place where Kerby
had first met Mrs. Graymalkin. It was there she had given
him the chemistry set. And it was there he had always met
her, except for the time when they were rescuing Waldo, the
night he disappeared. That time she had come along in her
old rattletrap of a car and given them a ride just when they
needed one most.

Seeing the park started a chain of thoughts going in Kerby's mind that led him to an inspiration.

"Mrs. Graymalkin!"

"What? Where?" cried Fenton, peering around.

"I don't mean I saw her, I mean I thought of her."

"Oh. What about her?"

"I'll bet she could help us!"

Fenton looked at him suspiciously.

"I mean, I'll bet she could help us beat Red Blake and his old Wildcats," Kerby went on.

"But that wouldn't be fair."

"Why not? Is bringing in a bunch of ringers fair? Listen, Fenton, we've got to fight fire with fire. Come on, let's go to the park."

Fenton trailed along as Kerby began his impulsive rush in that direction, but he did so grudgingly. Fenton was strict about always being on the up and up.

"It wouldn't be like when I got her to tell me a trick that would help me write a poem," Kerby argued over his shoulder as he tried to urge Fenton along. "I'll admit I was taking an unfair advantage that time, trying to win the first prize because it was an English bike — and look what it got me! Nothing but trouble. Mrs. Graymalkin taught me a lesson. But that was different. This time we're being taken an unfair advantage *of,* and all we want to do is fight fire with fire."

"Fire with fire. Well, maybe you're right," muttered Fenton, still wrestling with his conscience.

"Anyway, it won't hurt just to *ask* her. We can do that, can't we? Maybe she'll say nothing doing, and that will be that. You know how strict she is. She's as bad as you, when it comes to that."

Kerby had chosen his argument shrewdly. Fenton began to look happier about their mission.

"You're right. If she thinks it's not being fair, I'm sure she won't help us."

"Course she won't! Then what are you worrying about? Heck, we'll be lucky if she's even around, but at least we can look."

They entered the park and walked the length of it, past the drinking fountain and on to the most heavily wooded end. The whole park was full of trees, for that matter, and the trees were full of squirrels that Waldo loved to chase. Again, Kerby was sorry he wasn't along. Besides, Mrs. Graymalkin was fond of Waldo.

They looked everywhere, and even called "Mrs. Graymalkin!" a few times when nobody else was around. But she was nowhere to be found. After a while they sat down on a

park bench to rest, and Fenton began to apply his scientific mind to the situation.

"I think we're wasting time, Kerby."

"Why?"

"Well, just stop and think a minute. When is it you've always met Mrs. Graymalkin here, taking her constitutional?"

"Her what?"

"Her constitutional. That's what it's called when somebody takes a walk for his constitution, to get some exercise and keep in shape."

"Oh."

"When has it always been?"

"Well, let's see . . . Well, it's always been just about suppertime."

"Right!"

"Okay, what about it? It'll be suppertime before long now. So if we just wait around for a while, maybe she'll show up."

"But take a look around, Kerby. What did you see?"

"What a nutty question! I see trees and grass and stuff, same as anybody else sees in the park."

"I don't mean that. How did things always look when you met Mrs. Graymalkin? What time of day was it, besides being suppertime? Right now it's bright and sunny, and it'll still be that way at suppertime, because now it's summer. But when you met her here it was fall."

Kerby began to see what Fenton was driving at.

"You're right! Always it was beginning to get dark. It was dusk, and nobody was around, and everything was sort of . . . sort of . . ."

"Spooky?" suggested Fenton.

Coming from him, the mere word gave Kerby's back a tingle.

"That's right, but . . . Fenton! Don't tell me *you're* beginning to believe Mrs. Graymalkin is really a . . . a . . ."

Fenton laughed his scientific laugh.

"Certainly not. You know I don't believe in witches. But I do believe that Mrs. Graymalkin sort of likes to *pretend* she's one. I think that's why she always likes to pick that time of night for her constitutionals in the park. I just can't picture her walking along the path in broad daylight, like any ordinary person. No, sir. At this time of year, suppertime is too early, so what we've got to do is come back later, at dusk."

Kerby sprang to his feet.

"You're right! Let's go on home, and come back after supper, and maybe then she'll be here. I sure hope so, because we need help *fast!*"

They went home up Fenton's street, past Bumps's house. They found Bumps just putting away his lawn mower. They

54

had a short meeting in the clubhouse and reported on the Wildcats.

"Might know Red would try something like that," growled their president. But he glanced confidently at Fenton. "Well, let him! The bigger they come, the harder they swing and miss. Look at our game with the Cougars. Fenton only gave up three hits, we made five errors, and we handled four balls cleanly for putouts. Fenton's seventeen strikeouts took care of the rest."

Bumps shrugged.

"All Fenton has to do is strike 'em out that way tomorrow, and we'll beat them, even if they do have ringers in their lineup. So I ain't worried, and don't you guys be, either. Meeting's adjourned — I got to get cleaned up for supper."

Fenton was quiet until he and Kerby were walking on toward the fence.

"I didn't want to spoil Bumps's confidence, but gee, that's putting an awful burden on me," he declared. "Those Wildcats are no Cougars."

"Aw, if you've got your stuff, you'll make 'em roll over and play dead," said Kerby, trying to imitate Bumps's assurance. Fenton was awful good, but those guys were awful big. "Anyway, we won't take any chances. After supper, we'll go find Mrs. Graymalkin."

When they slipped through the fence and appeared in

55

Kerby's backyard, his mother pushed open the screen door and ordered Waldo outside.

"I wish you'd play with Waldo for a while," she told them. "He's been mooning around in here all afternoon, until it's getting on my nerves."

"Well, we've got news for him, Mom! Come on, Waldo! Hey, Mom, you know that big dog?" said Kerby, and told her what they had seen. She came out on the back stoop to hear about it.

"That's wonderful, boys. Now, if you can just get your message across to Waldo," she added, watching their household pet trudge down the back steps and walk lifelessly toward them.

"Can I go over to the park for a while after supper, Mom? I mean, may I?" said Kerby, catching his error before she could.

"Yes, I guess so, if you come home before dark."

"Thanks, Mom."

Mrs. Maxwell returned to the kitchen. Kerby, his hands on his hips, stared down at Waldo.

"There's got to be some way," he muttered. Then he brightened, and turned to Fenton. "Hey, maybe we could act it out for him! Maybe that would make him understand."

Fenton did not even ask for an explanation. He got the idea at once.

56

"Maybe so. I'll be the big dog, and you be the little one."

"Okay. Now, look, Waldo," said Kerby to their depressed friend, who was gazing up at them mournfully, "Fenton is the big dog. Watch!"

Getting down on all fours, Fenton hunched his shoulders up as much as he could and lumbered heavily across the grass.

"We should have got Bumps to do this, but I'll try," he muttered. He began to bark as deeply and thunderously as he could. "Ruff! Ruff! *Ro-o-o-w-wf!*"

"Not bad," said Kerby. "Get it, Waldo?"

At the sound of Fenton's imitation, Waldo had cringed down abjectly.

"He gets it!" cried Kerby. "He understands that you're being Gustavus!"

"So far so good," said Fenton. "Now you be the little dog, coming along."

"Okay. Now, watch, Waldo," said Kerby, getting down on all fours in front of him. "Pay attention. I'm a little toy bull terrier, a little bitty one, see?"

Kerby held his hands about a foot apart, to show how long he was, and about ten inches off the ground to show how high he stood.

"A real nothing of a dog, see, Waldo? That's me, now. Get it?"

Waldo cocked his head to one side in a noncommittal way, but at least he looked interested. Kerby began moving quickly along, back and forth on his hands and knees, making little yipping noises to show how small he was.

"Think he gets it?" he asked Fenton.

Fenton sighed.

"I'm not sure. But let's try. Okay, now, let me do a couple more barks, and then let's start walking toward each other."

Fenton went into his imitation again, causing Waldo to cringe once more, and then he and Kerby approached each other. Kerby took a look at Fenton, and lunged at him, yipping wildly. Fenton looked terrified and scrambled to retreat. He lifted his head and yowled in terror.

"Ow-wow-ooooooh!"

They stopped and turned to their audience.

"How about it, Waldo? Do you understand? That big dog was scared to death! He's nothing but an overgrown puppy, that girl he was with said so. All you have to do is growl at him once and he'll beat it!"

Waldo looked from Kerby to Fenton and back again, but without changing his expression. Fenton shook his head, discouraged.

"He thinks we're just trying to cheer him up."

"Waldo! Concentrate!" cried Kerby, seizing Waldo's head

and glaring deep into his brown eyes. "Come on, Fenton, let's try once more. Now, *watch*, Waldo!"

A moment later Mr. Maxwell drove up the driveway. He stopped without putting the car away, and leaned across the seat to watch the boys as they thumped about on hands and knees, howling and barking.

"What on earth do you think you're doing?" he demanded.

Both boys flopped on their sides, exhausted.

"Nothing, Pop," Kerby panted gloomily. "Darn it, how do you explain to a dog that he can stop worrying?"

7

BY THE TIME Fenton and Kerby returned to the park after supper, the pinks and light blues of a fine sunset afterglow had faded, and darker blues and violets had taken their place.

"This is more like it," said Fenton. Under the trees the shadows were deepening. The haze of dusk fuzzed the air and blurred the edges of distant objects.

"Just right for Mrs. Graymalkin," agreed Kerby. "I hope we find her."

Waldo was with them, but not by choice. In order to make him come, Kerby had been forced to get out his hated leash and actually drag him along for the first few steps. Waldo had finally given in, but he sidled along with a nervous air, looking this way and that, and almost getting under Kerby's feet in his effort to stay as close as possible.

"Darn it, Waldo, look out, will you?" Kerby glanced at Fenton. "He's afraid we'll meet Gustavus."

"I wish we would, with Buster chasing him."

"That's too much to ask."

The park was deserted at that hour. This was another good sign, because Kerby had never met Mrs. Graymalkin there when other people were around. They walked along the path past the drinking fountain. All at once Waldo whined and jumped forward, tugging on the leash. He led the way eagerly to a bend in the path. There, up ahead, just disappearing around the next curve in a flutter of black silk, was a familiar figure.

"Mrs. Graymalkin!" cried Kerby. They raced up the path. When they rounded the curve, no one was in sight. Ahead lay a long straight section of the path, but their friend had disappeared. They stopped and stared at each other.

"She must have gone like the wind!" said Kerby, with his spine tingling ever so slightly. "I don't see how an old lady can travel so fast."

"I'm sure there's some scientific explanation for it," said Fenton, with only the slightest quiver in his voice. "Let's go on, and —"

"Why, hello, boys! And dear little Waldo, how are you?" croaked a crackly voice behind them. They whirled to find Mrs. Graymalkin peering down at them with bright eyes twinkling in a face that was a network of wrinkles. A snaggle-toothed smile added to her merry air of being pleased with herself.

Mrs. Graymalkin looked well. The enormous feather trailing from her big squashy hat was as dramatic as ever. Instead of her draggly black cape, she wore a black silk shawl more suitable to summer weather, and her dress was also of some light material, but still black. Her shoes were the same high-heeled ones that had seemed so strange for such an old lady to be wearing when first Kerby had met her.

"How . . . ?" he began, astonished. "Where . . . ?"

"I was looking at a toadstool I happened to notice under the trees," she replied with a sly cackle. "Most interesting. Well, Kerby! Well, Fenton! And dear little Waldo! How have you all been?"

"Waldo hasn't been too well," replied Kerby, and explained what had happened.

"Dear me, that's too bad. But I'm sure everything will work out all right," said Mrs. Graymalkin, patting Waldo on the head. In his sorrow, Waldo ate up sympathy from any quarter. He responded by looking up at her piteously. Kerby wished he could have asked Mrs. Graymalkin if she could suggest something that might solve Waldo's problem, but he felt they had better concentrate on their larger problem with the Wildcats. After all, they could not expect her to take care of everything.

"We have a problem, too, and that's what we wanted to see you about. We're being taken advantage of."

"Oh? How's that, Kerby?"

"Are you a baseball fan, Mrs. Graymalkin?"

The enormous feather made great sweeps through the dusky air as she shook her head.

"No, I'm afraid I've never been caught up by our national pastime. A few hands of cribbage with an old crony is more my style — either that or exchanging recipes, though I don't suppose either of those is exactly what you'd call a sport."

"Well, that's all right. You don't have to know baseball to understand what we're up against," said Kerby, and launched into an account of Red Blake and his Wildcats. When he had finished, Mrs. Graymalkin nodded sharply.

"I see. You feel this Red Blake has taken an unfair advantage."

"I *know* he has."

"And you want something that will help you to be even better than his team is, with its unfair advantage."

"That's right!"

Mrs. Graymalkin laid a long, bony forefinger alongside her nose. Kerby thought of it as her thinking finger, because she always seemed to do that when she was thinking deeply. He and Fenton waited breathlessly while she thought.

Suddenly the finger was raised straight in the air.

"I have it!"

"Great!"

"First, though, tell me something. Do you have a container

of water at your games for the members of your team to drink? I suppose playing baseball makes one thirsty on a hot day, and tomorrow is going to be quite warm," she added.

"Sure!" said Kerby. "We always have a bucket of water. In fact, I'm the one that always brings it, because my mother has a bucket and a dipper she lets us use."

"Splendid," said Mrs. Graymalkin, "splendid, splendid, splendid. Now, then. You still have —"

"Yes," said Kerby eagerly. "I've got that chemistry set you gave me, but I couldn't find any trick in the thousand-and-one-tricks book that would help. That's why we came here looking for you."

"I see. Very well, then." Mrs. Graymalkin stared intently into space, consulting her memory. "What you need is a magic potion that will make you play better than you have ever played before . . ."

Kerby shot a delighted glance at Fenton and said, "That would be just right!"

"Yes, I don't doubt it would. Well, now. In your chemistry set, about the fourth or fifth tube from the right, is one on which you should still be able to read the inscription 'Flt.' "

"Flt?"

"Flt," she repeated, nodding. "F-l-t, Flt. And about six tubes from the left you will find one labeled 'Slp.' "

"Slp."

"That's right. S-l-p, Slp. I don't suppose there is much left of either Flt or Slp, so you had better use all of what there is of them. Pour them into a beaker and stir them carefully for one minute. Pour the mixture into an empty tube, cork it, and let it stand overnight before using."

"Overnight? Gee! That means we'll have to go home and mix it right away. And my folks are going to be home, because they're having some people over to play cards."

"One tablespoon in a bucket of water should be about right. But it has to stand overnight to be effective," insisted Mrs. Graymalkin.

"Then we'd better get going, and see if we can sneak down to the basement where I keep the chemistry set — er —"

"Hidden?" said Mrs. Graymalkin, supplying the missing word with a raspy chuckle.

"Er — yes," said Kerby, embarrassed. But then, he had never felt he could let his parents know he had the chemistry set, even though it was certainly not the dangerous kind with stuff in it that was likely to blow up, or otherwise do any harm.

"Well, you go along and do as I say, and I think you'll have what you need."

"Thanks, Mrs. Graymalkin!"

"And Waldo, I certainly hope you will be feeling better

the next time I see you," she said, patting his head again. "Now I must finish my walk. Goodby, boys! I hope to be enjoying my evening stroll here again tomorrow night, so do come tell me about your game then, will you?"

"We sure will!"

"Stroll, did I say? That is hardly the word for it, of course. In order to get any good out of walking, one must walk vigorously. Vigorously!"

Nodding approval of her own sentiments, Mrs. Graymalkin walked away up the path, teetering on her high heels but making surprisingly good time for such an old lady. Awed, they watched her vanish into the thickening dusk.

8

WHEN they reached Kerby's house, a car was parked out in front.

"The Bunthornes are here," said Kerby. "They're the ones that are going to play cards with my family tonight."

"Good. That'll keep them busy while we're busy."

"I hope so. But I'd like it better if my family was playing over at *their* house," said Kerby nervously. "I don't like to have anybody around when we're working with my chemistry set. You know how they'd probably act if they ever found out about Mrs. Graymalkin giving it to me."

"Especially if they saw Mrs. Graymalkin."

"Well, we can sneak in the back door and down to the basement —"

"No, we can't, Kerby. It's almost dark, and we're supposed to be in by dark. You'll have to tell your mother we're back."

"Then I'll have to introduce you to the Bunthornes, and all that stuff," sighed Kerby, "but I guess you're right."

The card game had not yet started when they came in. Mr.

Maxwell was just setting up the card table. Kerby introduced Fenton to the guests, and said they were going to fool around down in the basement for a while before Fenton had to go home.

"That's fine, boys," said his mother, and excused them.

"You're right, Fenton. Now we won't be bothered," Kerby admitted a moment later as they hurried down the basement stairs. They wasted no time on further conversation, but went to work in a businesslike manner. Kerby opened his toy chest and began shoving blocks out of the way to get at his chemistry set. Overhead, heavy footsteps came into the kitchen. He paused to listen.

"They're probably coming to get that pitcher of ice water," he decided, and began to lift out the chemistry set. But the footsteps crossed the kitchen toward the basement door.

"Put it back, put it back!" whispered Fenton sharply. Kerby began shoving blocks around to bury the box underneath them. The basement door opened, and his father and Mr. Bunthorne came down the stairs, laughing and talking about golf. Kerby was still covering the chemistry set with blocks. He finished as they appeared, but was too paralyzed by fright and his guilty conscience to slam the lid of the chest shut.

"I know that old set of golf clubs is down here somewhere," Mr. Maxwell was saying. Trying to look as nonchalant as

70

possible, Fenton had picked up a couple of the blocks and was balancing one on top of the other on the workbench.

Unfortunately Mr. Bunthorne was one of those people who notice children, instead of ignoring them. He glanced their way, and strolled over to peer into the chest.

"Why, what's this? Regular old-fashioned wooden building blocks!" he said, pleased. "I used to play with the same kind when I was a boy."

"So did I," quavered Kerby.

Mr. Bunthorne took a couple of blocks out of the chest.

"I used to build some great forts in my day," he declared. "By George, I'll bet I could still do it!"

"Go ahead," said Mr. Maxwell. "The ladies will take quite a while to look at that dress Pris made."

Almost before the boys knew what had hit them, Mr. Bunthorne was taking block after block out of the toy chest, building a fort on the workbench. And below the blocks, the chemistry set was coming to the surface. Its box was plain, old, and shabby, but in Kerby's scared eyes it seemed to be outlined with fluorescent tubes blinking on and off.

"I'll bet you've even got some toy soldiers," suggested Mr. Bunthorne, building away. He paused to tap the chemistry set. "Is this a box of them?"

Kerby was too frozen to reply at once, which was fortunate. It gave Fenton time to act.

"No, sir, his soldiers are in another box underneath," he said, and as coolly as could be, he bent over the chest, lifted the chemistry set out of the way, and put it aside on the floor behind the chest.

"This is your box of soldiers, isn't it, Kerby?" he said, pointing inside.

Somehow Kerby managed to unfreeze.

"Yes!" he cried, and almost dived into the chest to bring them out. He put the box of soldiers on the workbench and opened it for their guest. Mr. Bunthorne inspected Kerby's army with nostalgic pleasure.

"Now we've got something," he declared happily, and began to garrison his fort with a mixture of redcoats, cowboys, Indians, and World War II infantrymen.

"Where's that old popgun of yours, Kerby?" asked his father. "Does it still work?"

"Sure, Pop." Kerby kept everything and treasured everything, so that most of his old toys were still intact and in working order. He dug out the popgun and some corks.

"Attaboy!" said Mr. Bunthorne. "Let me put a few soldiers on the ramparts, and then I'll show you old Deadeye Dick in action."

He set up some soldiers so that no more than their heads and shoulders were showing over the wall, and stepped back a few paces with the popgun.

"Watch that Indian bite the dust." He cocked the gun and sighted fiercely along its barrel. Pop! The cork flew over the redskin's head and narrowly missed a redcoat. Mr. Bunthorne tried a couple of shots more, without inflicting any casualties.

"Gun must be erratic," he grumbled, examining his weapon critically. He thrust it at Kerby with a grin. "Let's see if you can hit anything, young fellow."

"Okay, Mr. Bunthorne." Kerby was so nervous about the chemistry set sitting right there on the floor out in the open that he could hardly pay attention to what he was doing. But then he didn't have to pay much attention, not with Old Trusty, the gun he knew so well. He drew a quick bead on the Indian, and this time the dust got bitten. Next he singled out an infantryman whose helmet barely showed above the wall, and sent him spinning.

"Young eyes, young eyes," sighed Mr. Bunthorne, shaking his head. "I'd hate to meet you in battle, my boy."

"Kerby, do you know where that old set of golf clubs is?" asked Mr. Maxwell, who had started to poke around in a corner. He even had to step over the chemistry set to get there.

"Yes, I know, Pop! Over here!" cried Kerby, and rushed toward a storeroom in another corner of the basement, where he knew the clubs were standing in their limp old canvas bag against the wall. He hurriedly brought them out.

"Look at these antiques!" Delightedly his father pulled

74

out an old wooden-shafted mashie niblick. "To think that I once shot a ninety-nine with these bludgeons!"

Ladies' heels clicked across the kitchen floor overhead. The basement door opened.

"What are you two doing down there?" called Kerby's mother.

"Looking at my old golf clubs and playing with soldiers," replied his father.

The ladies came downstairs to see, and there was great hilarity as they examined the fort Mr. Bunthorne had built, and took a couple of shots each at the soldiers, and generally enjoyed themselves while Kerby and Fenton stood by, dying by inches.

"Why don't we bring the bridge table down here?" Mr. Bunthorne suggested with a hearty laugh. "This is more fun than anything!"

The small groan that Kerby allowed to escape him was fortunately lost amid the grown-ups' laughter. By then they were all but standing in a circle around the chemistry set. Upstairs a bell tinkled. Kerby was never so glad to hear anything in his life.

"Oh, there's the phone," said his mother. "I'll get it."

"Well, I suppose we might as well all go, and leave the boys to clean up our mess," said Mr. Maxwell, and the foursome finally left them alone.

When the basement door had closed, Kerby sank weakly onto a stool and blew out a long breath.

"Whew! I never remember Pop bringing *anybody* down here before in the evening. Wouldn't you know that tonight they'd *all* come?"

The card game was safely under way upstairs, and the chemists were safely at work downstairs. They had experienced no trouble finding the tubes labeled "Flt" and "Slp." Flt and Slp were now mingled in a small beaker, and Kerby was carefully stirring the mixture while Fenton timed him.

Fenton looked up from his watch.

"Okay, that's one minute."

Kerby stopped stirring. They stared hopefully at the liquid in the beaker. There was not much of it, but there was more than enough.

"I'm glad it's colorless," said Fenton.

"Well, it would have to be, if we're going to put it in a bucket of drinking water!"

9

WHEN Fenton came over next morning, they had the house to themselves. Kerby's mother had gone out shopping.

"I found a box just the right size to carry the tube in," said Fenton, holding it up.

"Great. Let's go down and get the stuff."

Waldo followed them, but flopped down listlessly alongside the toy chest when he got there. Fenton stooped to scratch his ear.

"Cheer up, Waldo. You can't act this way forever. One big dog isn't the end of the world."

"*He* thinks so," declared Kerby.

He dug the chemistry set out of the toy chest. They removed the special tube and packed it carefully in the small box Fenton had brought along.

"You carry it," said Kerby. "It's safe with you."

"Okay," said Fenton, always able to shoulder an important responsibility. He put the box in his pocket, and they returned to the kitchen.

"I hope this stuff works all right," said Kerby, worrying.

"So do I," said Fenton, understanding his thoughts. "Those chemicals are pretty old. I wish we could test the stuff first."

"Want to mix a little in some water and drink it? I'll try it first and you can watch," said Kerby bravely. "You're more scientific."

"Well . . ."

Their consideration of this tempting idea was interrupted as the floor trembled beneath their feet and Waldo trembled at their side.

"RUFF! RUFF! RO-W-W-WF!"

"There's that darn dog again!"

Waldo cringed down, and gulped. His mouth must have suddenly gone dry with fear, because he skulked across the kitchen toward his water dish.

Kerby and Fenton turned to each other. The electrifying idea that passed between them did not even have to be put into words.

"Grab him!" cried Fenton.

Kerby pounced on Waldo. Fenton snatched up his water dish.

"Just a second, Waldo, we're going to give you some nice fresh water," crooned Kerby, holding him gently. "Don't put in too much you-know-what, Fenton."

"Only a few drops," promised Fenton, busy at the sink. In

a matter of seconds he had corked the tube again and returned it to its box, and was setting the water dish back on the
floor.

"RUFF! RUFF!"

"Never mind him. Have a nice drink," urged Kerby, letting Waldo go. Waldo gave him a confused glance, but continued on to his water dish and began slurping noisily. Outside, the barking continued.

"RUFF! RO-W-W-WF!"

Waldo paused, gulping down water. He licked his chops.
He straightened up. He listened to the barking.

His lips bared his teeth in a growl.

"Get the door open," said Kerby. Fenton hastened to hold
it open.

"G-R-R-R-RUFF!" barked Waldo, and sprang outside.

In Gustavus's case, it might have been enough had Waldo
merely come charging through the thin place in the hedge
without — this time — stopping. But to have a small dog come
leaping *over* the hedge was more than enough. Gustavus
took one look at the bounding bundle of wrath that was drop-
ping from the heavens, and began trampling underbrush for
all he was worth.

At the rate the dogs were traveling there was no sense in
trying to follow them. Kerby and Fenton stopped in the yard
and waited. High in a tree above them, Xerxes had looked

on goggle-eyed with amazement. Slowly he descended from his perch and sat down in his yard, staring in the direction the dogs had gone, listening to Gustavus's high-pitched howls fade in the distance.

After quite a while the conqueror returned. Trotting along with fierce glance and head held high, Waldo reentered his private territory. Seeing Xerxes, he stopped short. They eyed each other. Then Waldo let out a triumphant bark, and something very much like a joyous yowl came from Xerxes as the big yellow cat streaked for a tree with Waldo after him. In honor of the occasion they went around the tree four times instead of the usual three before Xerxes finally clawed his way up the trunk onto a branch.

When this ceremony had been concluded to the satisfaction of both parties, Waldo cleared the hedge again in a graceful leap, jumped up to lick Kerby's and Fenton's faces, and flopped down in the yard, once more the monarch of all he surveyed.

Kerby and Fenton exchanged a glance that was wild with surmise.

"Boy, does it ever work!" cried Kerby. "Wildcats, here we come!"

But then, by the time they gathered their bats and gloves together and started over to get Bumps, after lunch, Fenton was having one of his usual attacks of scruples. His conscience was bothering him.

"We'll put the stuff in the water, but we'll just take our chances on the other guys drinking any," he said. "It wouldn't be fair if we told them all to take a drink."

"And not only that, it would be fishy," Kerby pointed out. "They'd wonder why we wanted them to. And after they drank some they'd *know* why. But I'm not worried." Gaily he rattled the water bucket he was carrying. Inside it, the dipper clanked. "It's so hot today they'll all take a drink soon. I'm glad Mrs. Graymalkin was right about the weather."

Waldo was not with them. Afraid he might startle people with more leaps, they had left him at home. They had sneaked away while he was having a well-earned snooze on his personal rag rug in the kitchen.

Bumps came out loaded with his catcher's equipment.

"How's the arm today, Fenton?" he asked. He tried to sound casual, but it was easy to see he had been doing some reflecting and was less confident than he had been the last time they talked. Kerby hastened to reassure him.

"Don't you worry about old Fenton!" he said in ringing tones. "He'll show those Wildcats some pitching today like they never saw before!"

"I think I'll have my stuff, all right," was Fenton's opinion, which Kerby considered such a wildly funny understatement

82

that it was all he could do not to double up with laughter.

When they reached the field, most of the Wildcats were already there, practicing. A few of the Panthers were on the sidelines, playing catch to warm up and stealing worried glances at the team Red Blake had assembled. The Panthers' centerfielder, Joey Bush, rushed to meet them.

"Hey, Bumps, they got a bunch of big kids we never saw before!" Joey announced indignantly.

Bumps took a look, and almost gulped.

"Fenton will take care of them!" Kerby declared with the same sturdy assurance he had displayed earlier.

"Sure he will," growled Bumps. "You just worry about grabbing any ball that comes your way before it hits the ground, Joey, and belting a couple when you come to bat."

"Come on, Fenton, let's go fill the bucket." Kerby tried to sound as matter-of-fact as possible, but he was jumpy with eagerness to get their secret weapon ready.

"Okay, I'll walk over with you," said Fenton.

Red Blake had not missed their arrival, of course. He began to smirk, and waved to them from the sidelines, where he was warming up with the Wildcats' big catcher.

"All ready to pound our ears off, Bumps?" he called.

Bumps stared at him scornfully, and did not dignify his remark with a reply, probably because he could not think of a good one.

Kerby and Fenton dropped their bats and gloves beside the Panthers' bench and continued on toward the school building. On the far side of it was a faucet. Kerby was glad that was where it was located. They needed privacy.

While Fenton got out the tube, Kerby filled the bucket and set it on the ground.

"Pour it all in," he suggested recklessly.

"No, she said one tablespoon, and there's at least twice that much here. I'll use half of it."

Just as Fenton was finishing his task, sounds of whistling and of feet scuffing along made them start.

"Quick! Put away the tube!" mumbled Kerby. Fenton corked the tube and thrust it into his pocket an instant before Eddie Mumford came around the corner of the building carrying a bucket. He approached them jauntily.

"Hi, you guys. I'm glad to see you brought a big bucket. You're going to be plenty thirsty before *this* game is over."

"I expect so — from running the bases," retorted Kerby.

Whinnying skeptically at this remark, Eddie filled his bucket and turned to leave.

"I'm going to enjoy this!" he said over his shoulder as he strutted away. And when he reached the corner of the build-ing, they heard someone shout from the field, "Hey, Eddie, get the ball, will you?"

He turned again with a grin, and pointed.

"Look how far one of our guys hit it!"

Setting down his bucket, he ran out to retrieve the ball. Fenton and Kerby walked to the corner of the building for a look. The big catcher had been taking batting practice, and had hit one nearly all the way to the school building.

"Huh! He won't hit them that way off *you!*" said Kerby, turning to Fenton.

But Fenton was not looking at the ball. He was looking down at Eddie's bucket, and he had the tube in his hand. His face showed Kerby that once again he was wrestling with his conscience. But there was more than that in his expression. There was a bright-eyed fanatical curiosity about it that Kerby had seen before. It was Fenton's scientific look.

"Think what a game we would have if *both* sides . . ."

"Fenton! What are you doing?" cried Kerby.

Fenton had uncorked the tube. Water rippled as the Flt-Slp mixture spattered into it. The surface shimmered for an instant, and was still. When Fenton returned the tube to his pocket, it was empty.

"It just wasn't fair," he said. "And anyway, I couldn't resist the chance to see what happens when *both* teams play superball!"

Kerby was so shocked it took him a moment to recover. Then he was angry.

"Darn you, Fenton, do you *always* have to get scientific?"

He set their bucket aside and drew back his foot.

"Kerby, what are you doing?"

"Get out of the way! I'm going to kick over Eddie's bucket."

"Don't! Stop it, Kerby!"

Kerby's kick missed by an inch as Fenton grabbed him, and they fell to the ground, wrestling furiously.

"Let go of me!"

"No!"

Eddie Mumford came back for his bucket.

"You guys better save your strength for the game," he said. "You're going to need it."

The bucket handle squeaked as he strutted away. Kerby stopped struggling and banged one fist on the ground.

"Look at him, the smart aleck! I hope you're satisfied!"

Then Eddie stumbled over a root and almost fell. But he caught himself in time. Only a little water slopped out of his bucket. Kerby banged the ground again.

"Why can't we get a break just once?" he wailed.

"Why can't you be scientific just once?" said Fenton, still being fanatical about it. "We can play baseball anytime, but how often can we try something like this? This is even bigger than beating the Wildcats — and anyway, I'll bet we still beat them. Anything can happen now!"

"You said a mouthful that time," Kerby conceded bitterly.

He got to his feet and looked at their bucket. "Well, I don't know about you, but I'm going to drink some of this stuff right now. If anybody's going to be terrific today, *I* am!"

"No, wait a minute!"

"Now what?"

"Remember, Kerby, so far we only know how it works on Waldo. We don't know how it works on people. So let's let somebody else be the guinea pig."

"The what?"

"You know. When they experiment with something new in a laboratory, they try it out first on a guinea pig."

"Huh!" said Kerby impatiently. But at the same time, he hesitated.

"Think, Kerby. Remember what happened when you tried the lemonade trick?"

Kerby winced. He remembered, all right. *That* stuff had made him be a very, very good boy, which was a dreadful experience for any normal boy to have.

"And remember what happened when you tried the limerick trick?"

Again he winced. The stuff Mrs. Graymalkin told him about that time made him talk in poetry. Kerby stared somberly at Fenton.

"Don't you trust Mrs. Graymalkin?" he asked.

88

Fenton stared back at him. Then slowly they both began to grin.

"Come to think of it, neither do I!" said Kerby. "There's no telling *what* she might have up her sleeve. Maybe we'd *better* let somebody else be the guinea pig this time!"

"Now you're talking. Let's go."

Kerby picked up their bucket and they started back to the field. On their way they passed the place where Eddie Mumford had slopped some water on the ground. Fenton stopped and pointed.

"Look at that wet grasshopper. I wonder if he —"

The grasshopper jumped. Their eyes rolled up, up, up, and then down, down, down. They exchanged an awed glance.

"That's the biggest jump I ever saw any grasshopper make," declared Fenton.

"Me, too." Kerby stared down at their bucket. "Boy, does this stuff ever work!"

"For dogs and grasshoppers, anyway," agreed Fenton. "Now let's see about people!"

When they reached their bench on the first base side of the diamond, Bumps came over.

"Hey, get your glove, Fenton, and let's start warming up."

Anybody but Bumps would probably have wondered why his two friends began to stare at him as if he were something special. But if he had suddenly grown claws on his paws, two big front teeth, and a pink wiggly nose, he could not have been a more perfect guinea pig. Kerby set the bucket down carefully and made sure the dipper handle was hooked over the rim, nice and handy.

"Want a drink, Bumps?" he asked innocently.

"Sure, let me have some of that." Bumps reached for the dipper.

"I'll get my glove," said Fenton. "Come on, Kerby." He pushed his friend along in front of him, muttering in a low voice, "Stop watching him!"

Certainly it was not necessary to watch Bumps to make sure he drank plenty. All a person needed was ears, because when Bumps drank anything he was not polite about it. A lot of gulping and slurping went on.

They grabbed their gloves and came back. Bumps, with water dribbling down his chin, was watching a big bluebottle fly circle his head. Suddenly he swung the dipper at it.

"Got him! How's that? The old batting eye is all right today!"

Bumps swung at another fly.

"I can't miss," he declared complacently, and then looked down at the bucket. "Socko! Right in the old bucket, too! Look, I knocked a fly in the water bucket! Here, Jimmie, go get some fresh water," said Bumps, as he emptied the bucket on the ground.

90

10

BEFORE Fenton and Kerby could make a move to stop Bumps, the bucket was empty. They stared at each other, too stunned even to say anything. Not that there was anything left to say. Now the Panthers were really in for it!

As if they had read each other's minds, they both turned to look in the direction of the Wildcats' bucket. Had any of the Wildcats drunk from it yet?

The answer was yes — Moony Davis and Butterfingers Blatweiler, the two boys who were not getting a chance to play. The two cousins, Freddie and Ferdie, were taking their places again. Moony and Butterfingers were standing glumly beside the bucket, having a drink. Red Blake, seeing them, walked over and gave his whole team an order in his know-it-all way.

"Hey, you guys!" he shouted, looking around as the Wildcats came off the field from their pregame warm-up, "don't anybody start drinking any water till I say you can. If you're thirsty, suck a lemon. I got some in that sack there. I don't want anybody getting soggy from drinking too much water."

"When do we get to play, Red?" whined Moony.

"Wait till we're fifteen or twenty runs ahead, and then I'll put you in," Red promised easily, without sounding too sincere about it. He laughed. "You can pitch when I get tired, Moony."

"Aw, gee, Red!"

Meanwhile, Kerby and Fenton had brightened up a bit.

"We're all right for a while, anyway," murmured Fenton. "Okay, Bumps, let's warm up!"

While the Panthers were having their turn at fielding practice, Mr. Caldwell came walking over carrying his umpire's mask.

"All right, boys, let's get the game started," he said impatiently. "I ought to have stayed home and finished shingling my garage roof instead of coming over here, so let's get cracking, because I can't spend too much time."

The Panthers won the toss and got last bats. Kerby trotted out to his position at second base and watched Fenton warm up. Even without a drink of Mrs. Graymalkin's Feats O' Magic water, Fenton looked sharp. And one thing was certain: Bumps looked great. He handled his mitt like a big league catcher, and when he rifled a throw to second base after Fenton's warm-up pitches, he got off a perfect one. Kerby crossed his fingers and hoped for the best.

92

The game did not start well, however. Pinky Marshall led off with a single. Eddie Mumford hit one past Kerby for another single and Pinky went to third. Red Blake hit a double, scoring them both. With that, Bumps came out to have a conference at the mound with Fenton. Kerby listened in.

"Your curve ball is hanging, Fenton. We'd better try your fast ball."

Fenton looked down at the batter who was coming up to the plate. It was Pinky Marshall's big cousin. He was swinging three bats, and he looked seven feet tall.

"My fast ball? Against *him?*"

"Try it," insisted Bumps.

Fenton gulped, but he was game. His first pitch to Pinky's cousin was his fast ball.

Wham!

Pinky's cousin swung under it and sent a towering foul ball high and far behind the plate. Bumps tore off his mask and went after it while all but two of his teammates watched hopelessly. Bumps was not much of a runner. Ordinarily he could be counted on to stumble over his own feet within the first ten steps he took.

This time, however, he astonished everybody except Fenton and Kerby. Racing back and halfway up the embankment, he stuck out his mitt in a sensational effort.

Plunk!

"What a catch!" cried Mr. Caldwell, as the Panthers cheered. "By George, I'm glad I came over, roof or no roof!"

For a moment Kerby felt great. But then Cousin Freddie came to bat and hit a long double, scoring Red Blake. And Cousin Ferdie was up next.

They held another conference at the pitcher's mound.

"Give him the fast ball," said Bumps doggedly. Fenton sighed.

"Okay, I might as well. They seem to hit everything else I throw."

Cousin Ferdie let a couple of low pitches go by, and then swung at the next one. Again the ball seemed to go straight up, but this time it was a fair ball. It went so high that Cousin Freddie left second base and started toward third, sure that Kerby or the shortstop would drop the ball.

He had reckoned without Bumps Burton.

"Give me room!" yelled Bumps, thundering straight out toward second. He not only caught the ball, but beat Cousin Freddie to the bag for a double play.

Mr. Caldwell was so excited he had to pull out his bandanna handkerchief and mop his brow.

"An unassisted double play! Tremendous!"

"Aw, you must have seen a catcher make an unassisted double play before, Mr. Caldwell," said Bumps modestly as he came back to pick up his mask.

94

"Not very often, I haven't," insisted Mr. Caldwell, "and never at *second base!*"

With the score only 3-0, the Wildcats were out and the Panthers came to bat. And in the meantime the Wildcats' two bench warmers were becoming restless. They were warming up on the sidelines, throwing a ball back and forth. Sitting on the Panthers' bench, Kerby nudged Fenton.

"Look who's throwing straight."

"Yes, and look who's catching 'em!"

As a rule, Moony Davis could not throw a pitch ten feet in a straight line, and Butterfingers Blatweiler was a catcher who could not hold on to a ball if you handed it to him. But right now they were looking surprisingly good.

The first Panther batter struck out. Then Red got fancy with his curve ball, trying to catch the corners of the plate, and walked the second batter, Tommy Stern. Next Joey Bush rapped out a single, and that brought up Bumps Burton. Fenton and Kerby exchanged a glance of secret excitement. This was what they had been waiting for.

Bumps looked over Red's first pitch and didn't like it. But he liked the second one. He squared off and swung.

WHAM!

"Good, good," muttered Fenton in his scientific way. "The stuff is still working!"

While the Panthers danced on the sidelines, cheering his

96

tremendous home run, Bumps went hulking around the bases and crossed the plate behind Tommy and Joey. The score was tied, 3-3.

Over behind the Wildcats' bench, Moony and Butterfingers were still warming up. Moony was beginning to burn them in to his catcher. And his catcher was catching everything he threw. Moony yelled scornfully at Red.

"Any time you're tired, I'm ready."

"Shut up, Moony," Red yelled back at him.

"Hey, look at Moony!" called Eddie Mumford in an amazed tone of voice. "He looks great! Where did you learn to throw like that, Moony?"

"I've got my stuff today, that's all," snapped Moony, continuing to whip one good pitch after another into the expertly handled glove of Butterfingers Blatweiler.

What with Bumps Burton's home run and Moony's needling remarks, Red was so upset that he lost his control and walked the next two batters.

"How about letting someone pitch who can pitch?" jeered Moony.

"You shut up, Moony Davis, or I'll punch your head for you!"

"You and who else?"

"Just wait till after the game," Red promised him darkly, and hitched up his pants as he faced the next batter. The

Panthers' lineup was getting down to its weak end. Only Stevie Rizzo, Kerby, and Fenton had not yet batted. Stevie popped up to the pitcher, and it was Kerby's turn, with men on first and second and two out. Red threw him a hard one, and Kerby swung late. He hit an easy dribbler to Eddie Mumford, but Eddie fumbled it, and by the time he picked it up everybody was safe. The bases were loaded.

Red looked over at Moony Davis, who was still warming up and looking better every minute.

"Want to come in and put out the fire, Moony?"

"Sure! How about it?"

Red laughed sarcastically. "Are you kidding? With Fenton Claypool coming up?"

Everybody knew what a terrible batter Fenton was.

"Watch this, Moony, and take a lesson," said Red confidently, as he prepared to pitch to Fenton.

"Don't mind him, just meet the ball, Fenton," Bumps called from the bench, to remind Fenton of his batting lesson.

Red Blake turned and motioned to his outfielders.

"Come in close," he said, "or sit down, if you want to."

The fielders moved in. Fenton crouched at the plate, waggling his bat with pathetic ferocity.

"Straighten up and just meet the ball, Fenton!" yelled Kerby from first base. Nobody knew better than he just how

98

much Fenton longed to get a hit, but he also knew Fenton would never get one if he tried to kill the ball.

Red uncorked his first pitch, and Fenton's bat creaked through the air.

"Strike one!" cried Mr. Caldwell, jerking up his thumb. Kerby groaned. In his eagerness to really lambast one, Fenton was forgetting all about his batting lesson. The temptation to swing hard was too great.

Red threw again, and again Fenton swung.

"Strike two!"

Turning, Red motioned grandly to his outfielders.

"Closer!"

With lordly scorn, he hitched up his pants again and looked down at his catcher for the sign. Kerby was staring hopelessly at Fenton, and for an instant their eyes met. Fenton was panting. He looked desperate.

Then suddenly he backed away from the plate, gasping and coughing. He spit angrily on the ground.

"Darn! A gnat flew in my mouth!"

"Time!" called Mr. Caldwell, holding up his hand to stop Red from pitching.

His move back from the plate had brought Fenton close to the Wildcats' bench. And sitting on the ground beside the end of the bench was the Wildcats' water bucket.

Fenton helped himself to a drink of water. He spit some out, and then drank the rest of a dipperful.

"There, that's better," he said, and picked up his bat again.

An electric thrill zigzagged up Kerby's spine. He cupped his hands around his mouth.

"Okay, Fenton! Show 'em what you can do!"

Fenton settled himself in the batter's box again and swung his bat back and forth with slow, easy strokes, waiting for the pitch. Complacently, enjoying himself, Red wound up and let go with his best fast ball.

WHAMMO!

The leftfielder did not even bother to run after the ball as it soared high over his head. He just started walking, and he had a long walk ahead of him.

The Panthers on the bench exploded into the air, cheering wildly. Kerby rounded second and danced on over to third, looking back at Fenton. Moony Davis started walking out to the mound.

"Okay, now how about letting someone else pitch?" he demanded angrily. "Anybody that gives up a home run to Fenton Claypool hasn't got *anything* on the ball!"

But Moony had scarcely set foot on the field before Red came charging off the mound and rushed at him furiously.

"Get off the field! I'm running this team, and I'll show you —"

100

Before he could show Moony anything, Red found himself flat on his back from a push in the face. Meanwhile Freddie and Ferdie had come running in from the outfield to back up Red.

"You two guys trying to make trouble?" Ferdie wanted to know. He and Freddie looked as mean as a couple of gangsters.

Butterfingers Blatweiler stepped forward.

"Let me handle this, Moony. This is for Moony and me. We want back on our own team." With a spectacular leap, Butterfingers jumped straight at the cousins, seized each of them by the neck, and banged their heads together.

Two coconuts could not have given off a more satisfying *clonk*. And the sound was like a signal for all the other Wildcats to get into the fight. In a twinkling the ground was covered with threshing arms and legs, with squirming bodies locked in combat, as fists flew and elbows gouged ribs. While the Panthers stood by watching in amazement, the Wildcats fought their own civil war with Ferdie and Freddie taking the worst of it.

Meanwhile Fenton Claypool was trotting majestically around the bases, rounding third and coming home.

"Hey, where's home plate?" he said, brushing a couple of Wildcats out of the way with effortless strength. "I've got to score!"

102

Mr. Caldwell was so astonished by the rowdy turn the game had taken that he declared it ended.

"Game called!" he bellowed angrily. "I've got better things to do with my time than waste it on a bunch of hoodlums!"

Mopping his brow again, he turned to leave, stopping only long enough to have a drink of water. Then he started walking home across the field.

Now that he had crossed the plate, Fenton was thinking again, and he remembered something important.

"Kerby! We've got to save some of that water!"

Quickly he emptied their own water bucket, and together they ran around the edge of the battle.

"Everybody's watching the fight, nobody will notice us," muttered Fenton.

They were within five feet of their goal when someone gave Eddie Mumford a shove. He stumbled back out of the fray and sat down squarely in the bucket. Eddie got a very odd look on his face.

"Yeow!" he yelled. "That's *cold!*" And he fell over sideways, in a large, spreading puddle.

11

ON THEIR WAY home, Fenton and Kerby saw a couple of unusual sights.

When they passed Mr. Caldwell's house, he was already back at work on his garage roof. They had never seen a man nail shingles on a roof so fast. It looked as if he were spraying them on.

Then they passed old Mrs. Coogan's house. She was one of Bumps Burton's regular lawn mowing customers. When the game ended early, Bumps had decided to run over and mow her lawn for her. Not having his power mower with him, he was using her old-fashioned reel lawn mower, the kind with no motor on it. And he was pushing it so fast, and throwing up so much grass, that he looked like a boy running through a green blizzard.

"I wish we could have saved some of that water for more experiments," said Fenton, as he walked along balancing a bat on the palm of his hand. Of course, that was nothing special. Almost any boy can balance a baseball bat on the palm of his hand. The only difference was, Fenton was balancing a ball on top of the bat!

Kerby eyed him curiously.

"Listen, Fenton, did a gnat really fly in your mouth?"

Fenton looked at him with a sheepish grin.

"What do you think?"

"I think a pitcher will do anything to get a hit!"

Fenton looked guilty.

"I'm glad Mr. Caldwell stopped the game," he said, with his usual attack of scruples. "It wouldn't have been fair to win it that way."

"I suppose not," said Kerby, and sighed. "Darn it all, Mrs. Graymalkin's tricks are pretty good, but they never seem to work out right!"

Fenton thought this over. Then he chuckled.

"Yes, but they never work out wrong, either," he pointed out. "Just think of it! *I* hit a *home run!*"

THE BASEBALL TRICK is the fifth funny book Scott Corbett has written about Kerby Maxwell and his friends. The others are THE LEMONADE TRICK, THE MAILBOX TRICK, THE DISAPPEARING DOG TRICK and THE LIMERICK TRICK.

Mr. Corbett is the author of many other children's books, including the popular WHAT MAKES A CAR GO? and WHAT MAKES TV WORK? In addition, he has written several adult books and numerous articles.

A Midwesterner by birth, Scott Corbett now makes his home in Providence, Rhode Island, with his wife and daughter.

122741